D1525359

THE HIEROGLYPHICS

Michael Stewart

[m u d   l u s c i o u s   p r e s s   ]

first printing: 2011
cover design: Steven Seighman
editor: J. A. Tyler
assoc. editor: Andrew Borgstrom

author's note:

Horapollo Niliacus, who most likely never existed, wrote the original *Hieroglyphica*. It was a collection of some 189 interpretations of the Egyptian hieroglyphics, which were entirely, & unintentionally, fallacious. The collection was divided into two books, the first—the one I am using in the excellent Boas translation—dealt with 70 hieroglyphics & the second book with the remaining 119.

Using Horapollo's original chapter titles & order, as well as incorporating many of his sentences with my own, I have attempted to engage in a kind of conversation. To this end, I have also incorporated lines from the Book of Jubilees, the Book of Enoch & the Old Testament among others.

I apologize to Boas, Horapollo, & the ascribed writers of those other books for what I have done to their work.

isbn: 978-0-9830263-1-0
lccn: 2010942288

THANK YOU BRIAN,

THE HIEROGLYPHICS

Michael Stewart

1. { **Eternity** }

God is like a beast; he does not know time. To know time is man's alone, it is a weight only the seed of Adam may feel.

2. { **The Universe** }

It is the vast stretching. It is the smoothest, like water. It is ever coiling. The stars are just the shimmer of light off its scales. It is without end swallowing its own tail, its body resting in its mouth, its mouth resting on its body. It is ever watchful; when it blinks the sky darkens.

3. { **The Year** }

The first of their strange children born in a year is named & the year is given this same name. It is believed that the child & the year are one.

4. { **A Month** }

So each month there is a celebration & a new honor is given to her. Even the old women come to her on their knees & whisper requests. But when the last month comes, & winter begins to set on them, they stone the child, ending the year. Then prepare for the next.

5. { A Season }

The seasons are another of the Egyptians' tricks.
Their tax collectors with their knotted ropes sectioned
off the movements of the great bodies, as you might
separate horses or an enemy's spears. Still, the wind
drags its teeth over the five nations & the Nile satisfies
its hunger when it pleases.

6. { **What They Mean by a Hawk** }

The hawk does not rise or fall at a slant like other birds.
He plummets & soars. All stories refer to the one story.

7. { **The Soul** }

It is from heat that life comes. A lifeless body sealed from predators, but still exposed to the sun, will produce life, flawed & deformed maggots, but life. Our lips grow cold when we are close to death.

In the South there is a species of birds without mouths, which live only on the heat of the sun. At night these birds are so still they appear dead, but the heat from even a small fire is enough to make them stir & to blink their eyes, although it is not enough to allow them to fly.

8. { **Ares & Aphrodite** }

Our history & our future are written in omens & even the new beliefs cannot change this. Ares is followed by Pices, composed of Aphrodite & her son Eros. The Hunter always moves towards Leo whom he can never catch.

9. { **Marriage** }

When they speak of marriage they talk of crows nesting in an old woman's cunt.

10. { The Only Begotten }

Like the sons of Cain they are tender in their hatred
of God. Like glass they are only revealed when they
rebuke the light.

Since females do not exist among them they mix their
semen with warm clay & in this way fashion children.
Each father devises a son.

Sometimes they collect their spears & win wives. But
the women brought back wither quickly, their breasts
dry & from their folds tiny cocks protrude, which are
without semen & cannot grow erect.

11. { What They Mean by a Vulture }

These women have fashioned their own spears &
thus have no need for men. There are stories of them
descending from their city for a week every year &
engaging in great orgies. But those stories are not true.
When these women wish to fill their wombs they open
themselves to the North Wind & are covered by him
for five days. During this time they take neither food
nor drink, their only hunger being for conception.

They do not nurse their daughters on milk. Rather
they make deep cuts in their thighs upon which the
children are allowed to give suck. For this reason their
daughters are fearless: that blood is warm.

This tribe has warred with the armies of Alexander,
with the people of Cathay, against even the hordes of
demon-men to the West; they littered the hills with the
bodies of those giants. There are stories of the women
using the dead for pleasure. These are not true, but
the women do return to the battlefield; they bend over
those still moaning. They are quick with their knives.
They are the very opposite of pity.

12. { **Hephaistus** }

That tangle of a boy, all cock & legs. Broken fingers & oily hair.

13. { **What the Stars Signify** }

& by God the movement of the stars & the whole of the universe is accomplished. For apart from God nothing exists.

To read the stars is to know God's will. &, because time is unknown to God, our history as well as our future is written in the same script in that same book.

Our Horoscopist has learned that the movement of five determines the economy of the universe. Each night he notes the position of these stars, their waning & waxing magnitude, if they are covered by clouds, if their movement is forward or retrograde.

His notes are kept secret. Even the King may not know what is written in them. Divination without worship is an abomination. It is to not know time, which is an affront to God.

14. { **What a Baboon Signifies** }

Are not like other beasts who die in one day. But a part of them dies on each day for seventy-two days & is honored with funeral rites in the temples. Thus the temples have seventy-two rooms, & seventy-two Priests, each named after a part of the baboon.

15. { **Moonrise** }

The moon does not give off its own light, but borrows
the light of the sun & reflects it as if it were its own.
Such is the way with the good in men.

16. { **The Two Equinoxes** }

At the first point of Aries & the first point of Leo each
year the sun spends its time equally between earth &
heaven, which in large tells us the story of Hephaistus.

17. { **Spiritedness** }

Wrestling a lion, of the two testing each other against each other for many hours, neither finding in the other weakness. Hephaistus' form is said to have approached poetry. But what are fingers to claws; strong arms to such jaws? & who is to say the lion was not the Sun teaching the great Hephaistus humility?

18. { **Strength** }

To depict strength they draw the torn face of Hephaistus.

19. { **On Guard** }

We are awaiting the flood of the Emim, who our Priests
have told us are coming to drown the wickedness of
men, which is great on the earth. Man whose every
imagination of the thoughts of his heart is on evil
continuously.

20. { **Fear** }

We remove the fear from our daughters. If she is frightened of the dark then we tell her the night is full of jackals. We describe their teeth & the sound of their footsteps. In this way she learns to fear them more than the night. We push this; we make muffled steps outside of her tent until she is only tears & a fear of jackals. Until her trembling is four-legged. Only then do we offer her a spear & show her courage in a sharp point.

21. { **The Rising of the Nile** }

A tongue that extends from the stomach. Her always-
moist tongue. A tongue eager to taste mud & crops &
children.

22. { **Egypt** }

Egypt because with its heat gives life to all things in itself & by itself. From the mud of Egypt our children are made. From its terrible winds come our daughters. Egypt who is a drunken man & an insatiable woman. Who is so many shameful things.

23. { A Man Who Has Never Travelled }

God is more honest to the club-footed man, to the lame, to those with withered legs. He has written the limit of their steps into them. They are not pulled by the possibility. It is the sure-footed & the tireless who are taunted with the idea of the South.

24. { **A Phylactery** }

It is the custom of our spears to swallow a pebble before tying their sandals or painting their breasts, before the possibility of battle. This weighs down the soul, keeps it from escaping through their wounds too quickly.

Our children have their tricks too. They carve shapes into their arms. Hoping to impress the older girls with their ability to withstand pain, & hoping to entice the young spears to look at their long & well-formed arms. It is a way of saying that they are ready.

Even our old women attempt to control fate through little things. They dance in a crude fashion & chant & breathe smoke & other nonsense. As if God wished to look on their sagging breasts or hear their crooked voices.

25. { **An Unformed Man** }

Their misshapen hands make ungraceful children.
With huge, uneven arms. Overlarge heads balanced
on thin necks. Cocks as long as a child's arm extending
to the tops of their tiny calves. Thick fingers making
thick fingers & knotted ears. Wet eyes. The ungraceful
skin of frogs.

They are clay mockeries of a man. They are a
blasphemy & God hates to look on them.

26. { **An Opening** }

The bronze wall of Alexander has no opening. No
hinge. It is polished by the wind into a brilliant shine
& spans from one mountain peak to another.

On one side is written: *From here will the armies of Gog
& Magog, like a second flood, come to destroy the seed of
Adam.*

On the other: *This is the second cunt from which we will
spill.*

27. { **Speech** }

Hephaistus in his old age, after he had been driven from our cities in disgrace, went to the jungles of the East & there became a Prophet. One morning, when Hephaistus was making his body pure, a baboon appeared before him. Being perhaps mad, the old man began to reveal the secrets to the mute baboon. At the end of the first year the baboon repeated back one word to the old teacher. & so Hephaistus taught the baboon for four more years until he had revealed to his student the greatest mystery. The baboon then went among his kind & taught them how to make these words & so it happened that the great mystery was not lost.

When Hephaistus died, the first baboon waited the five days of mourning & then descended into the cities of man & was captured. The baboon was taunted & kept in a cage & people paid to look at him, but the baboon did not utter a sound. Until one day a Priest walked by & saw how the beast was being treated. Moved to sympathy, the Priest purchased the baboon. Later that night the mystery was revealed for the first time in a generation of men. & so the temples were built.

28. { **Silence** }

On the forty-third day the baboon's tongue dies. In the morning it begins to lose color & by evening it has withered into a wrinkled, stiff leather, which the Priests solemnly remove. For this reason silence is also referred to as the baboon's black tongue.

There is more to say about silence. A dumb man is considered neutered because birth was the first function of the mouth, until the second day when Adam's original mouth was given to Eve. Even today the act of speech mimics that of coitus. The tongue makes the mouth's womb productive. Our mouths still ache for their first divine function & it is for this reason that we receive so much pleasure when a tongue parts our lips or a mouth swallows our seed. God loves for like to meet with like.

29. { **A Distant Voice** }

Is what pulls our young men over the desert. Every year two or three of them go to the South. They lay down their spears & they do not take with them any food.

Their mothers are in the habit of burning a sparrow on the night they leave. The hope is that the ghost of the sparrow will follow the boy. How this sparrow will protect them we cannot imagine, but maybe these little things are enough.

They do not come back. Certainly they die looking for that voice. Perhaps they grow weak & are killed by feral dogs, or perhaps after so many days their legs buckle & they fall gracelessly into the sand, the voice just a little distant, & die there listening. Perhaps, however, they do find something.

30. { **Ancient Descent** }

We know that all things do not come from God,
certainly not the ever-wet tongue of the Nile or the
indifferent North Wind. Aberrations are the progeny
of sin & God is sinless. Thus, we cannot weigh the
blame of our birth onto God.

We are bastards. There, it is said. We are the adopted
sons. Our fathers unknown; our mothers look away
when they see us, they pretend not to recognize
their sins. For this reason we are of the most ancient
descent. The first son was a bastard, the first daughter
an unwanted harlot. But this neglect has been good
for us. It has made us hard & when the time comes we
will be our own midwives. Our terrible birth will kill
our mothers in their attempts to keep us in. Our first
cries will be battle cries. We will not be casual in our
hatred nor negligent in our revenge. Our fathers will
know us.

31. { **Taste** }

The mouth & the ass are both tools of the same function, but they must be kept distant for the health of the body. So it is with Holy Men & Spears.

The function of the mouth is to take & to discriminate. The Holy Man must taste the words he is given & sort the bitter from the sweet, & give to the body each in measure.

The function of the ass is to clear the body of impurities that have made their way in. & it is not for it to discriminate.

32. { **Pleasure** }

It takes sixteen years for our sons to learn this secret & fewer years for our daughters. It becomes an ever present buzzing in the ears, a reminder. Like the other mysteries, the seeds of it have always been present & at its realization it seems inevitable.

33. { **Copulation** }

But what comes naturally should be augmented with learning. On their fourteenth year our girls are taught the thirty positions & their names. When they are performed correctly & in the proper order it is said that the sacred text is rewritten. The bodies form hieroglyphics & the reading forms bodies.

34. { **The Soul Delaying Here a Long Time** }

Hesitancies suffer a species of damnation unknown to any other sin.

Some souls are not quick, are heavy & cannot, like smoke, lift up to God. But yet are not so heavy that they mix with the mud & become again men. These souls rest against the ground like dew, which during the day rises only to fall during the night. This is their fate, until the world ends & all things on it end.

So, if a man should be good, let him be great. But if a man should be evil, let him have no pity, let not the least good touch on him.

35. { **The Return of the Long-Absent Traveller** }

An old man came to our camp in the blush of evening. He walked easy & was standing straight. He was missing one ear & several fingers, each cleanly removed. In response to our questions he opened his mouth & past the crooked, grey teeth we could see that his tongue as well had been removed. We were curious & brought him food proper for an old man. After eating he scribbled in the ground for awhile with his knotted finger. Most of the writing was illegible, the characters were the shaky script of a child, but two words could be read. First *son* & then, much later in the writing, *flesh*. We pressed questions at him & he ignored them like you would a gnat. I am unsure he could even understand what we were asking. Soon we withdrew our questions & sat with him in silence.

He fell asleep leaning against a log we use as a hitch. When he slept he made a garble of noises more suited to an animal than to a man. He woke several times in a panic, but clammed quickly & slipped back to sleep.

When in the morning he collected the articles of his small bag & began to walk from us we did not restrain him, because we did not recognize him.

36. { **The Heart** }

The heart is many chambered like a temple because it is the home of the soul.

When the bodies of the fallen are too great & cannot be carried back to be buried in observance of the law & God's will, which are two that are one, their hearts are brought instead & buried with all ceremony afforded to them. This is because it is the soul only which we honor. The body is a thing for maggots & vultures. & God thinks that this is good.

37. { **Education** }

It is our hope that we might teach our sons to avoid the
pursuit of knowledge & keep instead to the pursuit of
God & the Holy & how the Holy may be found in the
five words or a spear. It is a curse to have a son who
questions. Questions are the refuge of the impotent.

38. { **Egyptian Letters** }

The Egyptian letters are thin little sticks, more suited to counting than to the noble art. Their scribes tried to write down the mysteries. The story of Hephaistus. But you cannot do this with the letters of a tax collector. It is impossible.

39. { **The Sacred Scribe** }

The Sacred Scribe instructs our daughters. She teaches them first the ways they are to bend their bodies & then how to guide their husbands into the gaps. In this way it is shown that one's shape has no meaning without the other. She then teaches them the necessities, how to collect the blood & to make the body ready.

She teaches them what is forbidden. Just as the words of a fishmonger are not pleasing to hear from the mouth of a woman, so are common movements kept from the mouth of God.

She teaches them the quiet language of their bodies. The prayers of food, which are made with their fingers. The daily prayers that are accomplished with their breathing. The prayers of fecundity, which are spoken with the movements of their eyes. & the prayers of women, which even a husband may never see.

40. { **The Magistrate or Judge** }

The astrologers, conjurers, witches, heretics, & diviners, who had once been Wise Men, were pulled before our judges on that day & their rod & stole were taken. Once their cases were heard they were offered the right hand. If they refused we brought sharp, hot points to one of their eyes, making their sight of this world imperfect so that they might better see the way of God. Again they were offered the right hand. If again they refused, they were no longer accounted among men; they were stripped & treated like dogs. Fed scraps & beaten when their howling became a nuisance.

41. { **The Shrine-Bearer** }

What we hold holy we keep in a shrine one & a half cubits in height & in length. When we go to battle it marches before us. We choose a young boy who has yet to know battle & to him the shrine is entrusted. It carries him to battle.

42. { **The Horoscopist** }

Is a man honored by us. The only one of the Wise Men
who could still wear the stole, carry the rod after the
temples were built. He is honored because he feeds us
our hours. It is he who we trust to sift & drop the sand.
He who has been given the knotted rope to measure
our plots & to section off the movements of the great
bodies. He who can read our history & future in the
five stars.

43. { **Purity** }

The Catorin makes men pure.

Before the temple doors will open to a hopeful he must for thirty days fast & partake of the Catorin.

Its petals are a thick yellow with threads of red. Its blossom is too large so when it blooms the rest of the plant dies.

An older Priest will come & present the Catorin to the hopeful. It rids the body of the things that a man needs to live. It makes the lips tingle. It sometimes causes the gums to bleed & the teeth to become loose.

The Catorin pulls men close to God.

Some Priests scar their faces before approaching God, because it is said that he keeps the beautiful ones next to him.

Sometimes the uncomprehending body will spit out the flower, its petals sticking to parched & bloody lips. At these times the older Priest assists the hopeful. He presses the flower back with a finger & massages it down the hopeful's throat with gentle movements.

On the thirty-first day the hopeful is made pure. If he wakes, he is walked into the temple to be taught the five mysteries. If not, a priest bends over the body & he whispers the five words, a bell sounding with each word so that none should overhear. & he is buried, his lips painted the black of a Holy Man. His left hand closed into a fist.

44. { **The Lawless or the Abominable** }

It is the law & speech & the knowledge of time that
separate beasts & men. Thus, a man incapable of these
is not a man. The dumb are denied a woman, which
is the right of any whole man. The lawless & caged
are treated with disgust like feral animals. The man
who does not know time is an affront to God, an
abomination. His hours are purgative & eat each other.

45. { **The Mouth** }

It is said that God, with the mercy only known to the powerful, offered salvation even to the bastards of Gog. That he said to them:

You who are the progeny of Semjaza, whose birth was a blasphemy, you I will give navels & teach the proper way of making flesh. If you call me father I will extend to you this covenant: I will clean your hands that you might make temples. I will correct your misfigured faces that I should be pleased to look on you. & if you will chase the beasts from the sacred places I will teach you to make altars & prayers. I will move the tongue of one of your sons that you may learn my laws.

To this the bastards of Gog replied with the murder of the men of Kay, with the desecration of their temples, the rape of their wives, & the theft of their sons. War is the language of the Gog. Their spears are their tongues & the wounds they inflict are their hundred mouths.

46. { **Courage with Temperance** }

The first jackal that they put to the spear introduces them to the warmth of courage & like a body long cold they wish to stay next to it, to coax it & watch it grow.

They shout. They push & swing their spears wide. They roll their hips when they walk by their elders. We allow this to make sure their embers are strong. Then we teach them that there are things stronger than jackals, things that cannot so easily be killed.

We turn them away from our fires & deny them food. This does not bother them; they make their own camp not far off. But soon they drift back towards our laughter & dancing. When they enter our camp we beat them, as you would a dog begging for scraps. Over time their pride wears thin & they come to us grovelling, petitioning forgiveness for their arrogance. If they are sincere, forgiveness is granted & they come to us girls no longer, but women.

47. { **Hearing** }

The ear is shallow & may only hold little.

48. { The Member of a Fecund Man }

The member of a fecund man is removed upon his death & allowed to dry until it may be ground into powder. This powder is mixed with the fat of a goat.

When a boy wishes to become a man his cock is treated with this oil & made to stand erect. His foreskin is removed. When he recovers, he may present the foreskin to whichever woman he chooses. If she accepts, she is taken to the Sacred Scribe & taught those secrets. If she refuses, he is given a spear & is wed to it.

49. { **Impurity** }

He taught that it was good for the Holy Man to take impurity into the body so as to prevent the tribe from infection, that his lips should be black with sin, that men were made for sacrifice. & in his age he breathed in sin like a Magog witch breathes in smoke. He cut his hair in the manner of a slave. He pissed in the Temple. Disfigured a Wise Man. He polluted the children & sold his daughter for the pleasure of goatsmen & soldiers.

We were disgusted with him. His scalp was full of scabs & he had withered into this, but when we went to arrest him he proved he was still Hephaistus. Men died that day. He used his teeth & hands & the jagged end of a stick. He taught our men the lessons that he had learned from the lion & our men died accordingly. Eventually we broke him with arrows & drove him from the city, but the victory was tasteless. When you kill a god you must also kill the part of you that had believed.

50. { **Disappearance** }

On the fifth day of the fifth month, when the Priest went to open each of the sacred doors, they discovered that the baboons had left. Each mutilated body had clung to the next & had managed to make two legs of their parts. The Temple was full only of the smell of piss & fur.

Immediately men were sent to the forest with nets. But those that they brought back struggled in their cages like beasts & could not be induced to say the five words. When they were cut they bled & bellowed in the manner of animals until they died.

51. { **Impudence** }

A man may invent many ways to sin. Just as through a forest a man may make many paths, so might a man invent many ways to sin. There is only one end, but the means may multiply.

A man standing pure before the altar is an affront to God. Better that he prick himself with some little sin, let it bead at the end of some vice. As a blemish on the face of a beautiful woman is pleasing, a single flaw is prudent, the man humble & God appeased.

52. { **Knowledge** }

Each thing a man knows about this world distracts him from God.

53. { **A Son** }

We have hopes that we bury, as you might bury a coal in sand only to resurrect it when it is cold. That one of our sons might return is one of those hopes.

He would be given to the tribe, a son to each of us who has lost a son.

Our Wise Men tell us that a man is worth a pound of flesh. & so we have collected this tax. Each father giving a finger from his right hand. We made the offering into smoke & our Wise Men made our prayers.

54. { **A Fool** }

Each man joining purpose & becoming one fool.

55. { **Gratitude** }

We said, if He would grant us this, we would make prayers & burn incense. In our gratitude we would become better men & make the Lord pleased.

The years passed; our prayer, we thought, had been forgotten. Our sacrifice rejected. We nursed our wounds & spite.

But he did come. Ten years after our prayers, our eyes then too dim. Our scars too dull to remind us. This is how short the memory of man is. This is how low & ungrateful. We know that.

56. { **The Unjust & the Ungrateful** }

The unjust & ungrateful are called before God & He says to them:

I gave you arms & you raised them to try your sire. I gave you lips & with them you gave birth to blasphemies. So, I will have them back.

& the arms of the ungrateful are torn from their bodies & the lips of the unjust are cut from their faces.

I gave you eyes that you might see my wonders & believe, but when I gave you back a son that you might know my love, you did not see him. So, I will have them back.

& one-by-one the gifts of God are returned to him until what is left is all that a man is worth.

57. { **Ingratitude for Kindness to Oneself** }

A scar is the body's way to remember, it is a kindness given by the Lord to remind us of what happens to the ungrateful.

58. { **The Impossible** }

It is impossible for a man to give birth to himself or
to lift his body from the ground. It is impossible for a
man to stand on water like firm ground. Impossible
for a lion to speak other than with claws & teeth. The
list of impossibilities is long & reminds us how pale
are the achievements of men.

59. { **A Very Powerful King** }

Of the five kings this king is the least of kings, but for that he is the most terrible. Like a young lover he has yet to learn the value of stillness.

This the least of kings is waiting for death with 40,000 soldiers & very tall walls. Death will have to wage a war on men to take him & even if Death can penetrate the great walls & the greatest army still he will have to be nimble, the old king is quick. His fury is like the wind. He is virile. Even his hate is sharp. He is our king.

60. { The King as Guardian }

The King is to his people as the soul is to the limbs. He guides their movements so that they reach harmony with the body. He protects them from harm for the good of the body.

61. { **A Cosmic Ruler** }

But it is better that a hand were cast off than that
harm were brought to the soul. The King is himself
subservient to the Cosmic Ruler, He who gave us
language & taught us the laws & visits with both
blessings & judgments.

62. { The People Obedient to the King }

It is good for the body to obey the soul. It is good for the soul to obey the Lord.

63. { The King Ruling Part of the Cosmos }

Such is how God has organized the universe. That God is to the King as the King is to the People. As the People are to beasts.

64. { **The Almighty** }

When the end comes greatly with giants & droughts. I
have seen. Our sins will become boils & the stench of
our ingratitude will thicken & spill & spoil from our
mouths. There is not one man among us who will sit
comfortably in his home. The end will come greatly.
Men will shave their heads & build altars & make
prayers. But His ears will be closed. His pity spent. He
will show us his left hand & no man will be spared.
He will come as maggots & infertility & fever, mold,
disease. Greatly.

65. { **A Fuller** }

We take our piss in the Fuller's vat that he might scour
the cloth. His bare feet pressing & then thickening the
wool. Sometimes he is still, the mound of cloth just
below the surface so it seems as if he is standing on
piss as if it were firm ground.

When the Fuller is buried we remove his feet at the
ankle that the smell may not follow him & displease
the Lord.

66. { **A Month** }

Is depicted as a bull in the Egyptian language, because at the beginning of the month the moon raises its horns & at the end of the month it lowers them.

67. { A Plunder, a Fecund Man, a Madman }

He has in turn been called each of these things. He has also been a prophet, warrior, & our goat. He has been our father, great & terrible. The wall that secured us against the coming Emim.

His body appeared outside of our walls ten years after we had driven him from the city. He was old but not aged, the old scars were still visible, but seemed somehow subdued. Whoever had brought him had made him ready for death. His hair had been combed & parted. His mouth filled with salt, his left hand closed, the nails cleaned & cut. His skin was washed, his clothes new. He was as perfect as the First Man.

We chose the ground & set fire to it & then mixed salt with the earth so that once we buried him nothing should gain from his death. We checked his palms & they were without calluses, so he was not given a weapon.

68. { **The Rising [Sun]** }

With the rising sun we opened our doors & windows
& let the cold in, that our bodies might know our
grief. We lit torches with the first light & made circles
around his body & kept the silence.

69. { **A Sunset** }

When the sun began its decline we began to lower
his body. & the forest woke & shook with a strange
screeching. The birds made odd shapes in the sky. The
crocodiles left their beds & came to us docile. We were
frightened by these signs, but kept the silence.

When the dark came we met it armed with our torches.

70. { **Shadows** }

& the shadows did not grow that night. When we covered the face of Hephaistus, our Holy Men chose their words & brought calm to us. *Each day,* they told us, *His book is written in omens. He speaks to us in things because his voice is physical.* & then they read His signs for us. & their last words to us were these, *There are plenty of other meanings of the nature of a crocodile, but this will suffice for the first book.*

M i c h a e l   S t e w a r t is currently the Rhode Island Council for the Arts Fellow in both fiction & poetry. His work has appeared in a variety of journals & anthologies including *Conjunctions*, *Denver Quarterly*, & *American Letters & Commentary*. He is the author of *A Brief Encyclopedia of Modern Magic* (The Cupboard), *Almost Perfect Forms* (Ugly Duckling) & *Sebastian*, an illustrated book for adults (Hello Martha Press). He lectures at Brown University.

[www.mudlusciouspress.com]